Tales from Mossy Bottom Farm

FLOCK TO
THE SEASIDE

Copyright © 2015 by Aardman Animations Ltd.

First U.S. edition 2015

Library of Congress Catalog Card Number 2014951550
ISBN 978-0-7636-8058-9

15 16 17 18 19 20 BVG 10 9 8 7 6 5 4 3 2 1

Printed in Berryville, VA, U.S.A.

This book was typeset in Manticore.
The illustrations were created digitally.

Candlewick Entertainment
An imprint of Candlewick Press
99 Dover Street
Somerville, Massachusetts 02144

visit us at www.candlewick.com

Tales from Mossy Bottom Farm

FLOCK TO THE SEASIDE

Martin Howard

illustrated by Andy Janes

CANDLEWICK
ENTERTAINMENT

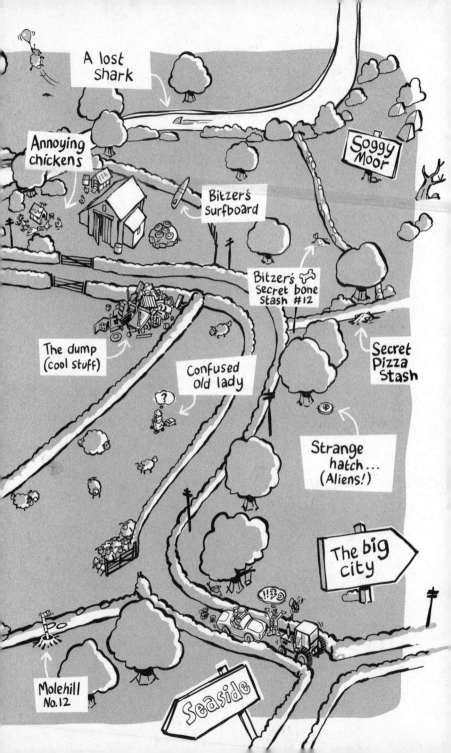

SHAUN is the leader of the Flock. He's clever, cool, and always keeps his head when the other sheep are losing theirs.

BITZER

The Farmer's faithful dog and a good friend to Shaun, Bitzer is an ever-suffering sheepdog, doing his best to keep Shaun's pals out of trouble.

THE FARMER

Running the farm with Bitzer at his side, the Farmer is completely oblivious to the human-like intelligence—or stupidity—of his flock.

THE FLOCK

One big happy (if slightly dopey) family, the sheep like to play and create mischief together, though it's usually Shaun and Bitzer who sort out the resulting messes.

TOP DOG

With his Top Dog hat and eHerder device, Top Dog is the best sheepherder in the business— and he knows it.

TERRY THE POO BEETLE

Terry's a lovely little beetle. He's not actually in this story, but his mum won a competition for him to appear in the new Shaun the Sheep book.

CONTENTS

CHAPTER ONE

BIG DAY OUT

In the trailer behind the Farmer's car, Shaun and the Flock bounced along green and leafy country lanes on a hot summer's day. As swallows dipped and swooped around them, the sheep bleated and hung their heads over the sides of the trailer, enjoying the breeze and taking in the sights of the open road.

Shaun's favorite sight was the Farmer's bald head banging against the roof of the car to shouts of "Ooo-aaaargh!" and "Bah!"

every time the car hit a bump in the road. Beside the Farmer was Bitzer, his head sticking out the window and one paw on his hat to keep it from blowing away. His tongue fluttered in the wind like a pink flag.

Shaun held on tight as the wheels hit an especially big bump. The Flock bleated to one another. With every mile, their curiosity grew. Where was the Farmer taking them on such a beautiful day?

Timmy was dreaming of the seaside. Shirley hoped they were going out to lunch at a restaurant with a dessert cart so large that it took three waiters to push it. The Twins wanted to go to a rock festival to see their favorite band, **THE REVOLVING CUCUMBERS.**

Nuts was sure they were going to the theater. He'd even brought some chocolate-covered raisins he'd found sprinkled over the floor of the rabbit hutches to share during the intermission. He peered into the paper bag. The rabbits were crazy to leave perfectly good chocolate-covered raisins lying around like that.

Nuts's thoughts were interrupted by an excited bleat from Shaun, who was leaning over the side of the trailer and pointing a hoof. Through a gap in the trees, Nuts caught a glimpse of something that was deep blue, sparkling, and dotted with white. The Farmer wasn't taking them to the theater.

He was taking them to the seaside!

The Flock bleated delightedly as the car clanked over the top of a hill. The sea spread out before them, stretching to the horizon. Even better, in the distance were the striped tents, Ferris wheels, and roller coasters of an amusement park. The breeze smelled of cotton candy and sunblock.

Squeezing his eyes closed in concentration, Timmy reached into Shirley's fleece and pulled out a bucket and shovel. Reaching in again, he found a pair of floaties and a surfboard. Happy sheep beamed at one another. Shaun started three bleats for the Farmer: "Bleat, bleat-ooo-ooooo . . ."

The second bleat turned into a wail as the car turned sharply. The Flock was thrown from one side of the trailer to the other and almost tipped out. Then, on two wheels instead of four, the car screeched through an open gate and skidded to a halt in a field.

"Bleat," finished Shaun in quiet disgust.

The meadow was filled with familiar sights. Farmers in muddy green coats and tall rubber boots stood sipping tea and eating sandwiches outside a small tent. Through the open flap of another tent, Shaun could see men poking an enormous squash and making notes.

There were stalls selling **BARRY STILES'S SHEEP DIP** and **HOOF-U-LIKE OINTMENT** and **DOCTOR ULCER'S PIGGIN' LOVELY PIG RUB**. A sign that read **THE GREAT PIDDLINGTON-ON-SEA ANNUAL FARM EXTRAVAGANZA** hung from the front of a trestle table, behind which sat three judges with matching hats.

In the center of it all was a large green space dotted with hurdles and pens.

The Flock peered over the side of the trailer and groaned. They weren't going to the seaside after all. The Farmer had brought them to a farm show, and that could only mean one thing: a sheepdog trial!

There wasn't even an ice-cream truck.

Meanwhile, the Farmer had spotted the tea tent. "Oooyumnumnum," he cried, rubbing his hands together. Glancing toward Bitzer, he jerked his thumb over his shoulder toward the Flock and barked an order before striding away, licking his lips.

Bitzer jumped out of the car, clipboard in paw. He paused to stare dreamily at the largest of the gold cups on the judges' table. He had heard about this trial. It was legendary among sheepdogs. Only the best—the *very* best—could hope to win the **GREAT PIDDLINGTON-ON-SEA ANNUAL FARM EXTRAVAGANZA GOLD CUP FOR BEST SHEEPDOG.** A look of determination crossed his face. This time, the cup would be his.

But first he had to prepare. He unhooked the back of the trailer and blew his whistle, ordering the sheep out into the field. He tapped the clipboard with his pencil as they shoved and jostled around him. In a moment he would direct them to a holding pen to wait their turn, but now he needed to take them through a few tactics and practice moves.

Bleating and sniggering, Shaun held up a hoof. Would these be like the tactics Bitzer used at the last trial, when he had tried to impress the judges by wearing roller skates and had herded the sheep straight into a Porta-Potty.

Bitzer scowled, remembering how he had also skated through a cow pie, accidentally splattering it all over the judges. Ignoring Shaun, he showed the sheep the clipboard. At the start of the course, they would form Bitzer Herding Formation A and then proceed in an orderly fashion to —

Scornful laughter interrupted him.

Bitzer turned around. Behind him a dog in a **TOP DOG** baseball cap leaned against a holding pen that contained sheep in perfectly straight lines. Each sheep had an electronic device clipped to one ear. In one paw, the dog held a gadget that looked like a cell phone. He also had an expensive-looking earpiece and microphone. His eyes were hidden by mirrored sunglasses. Chuckling, he shook his head at Bitzer's clipboard and tapped the screen of his device.

Bitzer's jaw dropped as a fizzle of electricity went through Top Dog's sheep. With a startled bleat, they all jumped into a perfect circle. He tapped again . . .

Top Dog tapped a final time. His flock all leapt back into straight lines. With a sneering bark, he flashed his phone at Bitzer. Clipboards and whistles were *soooo* old-fashioned. *Everyone* had an eHerder these days. It made herding simple, plus it could be used as a telephone and a camera . . .

Bitzer looked as though he'd been electrocuted too. Seconds passed as he stared, mouth hanging open, at the eHerder, until Top Dog snickered again and pointed over Bitzer's shoulder.

Bitzer tore his gaze from the gadget and glanced back at the Flock. They were . . .

With a gulp, he turned around slowly and blinked.

. . . they were *gone.*

CHAPTER TWO

HERD ON THE RUN

Bitzer tried to bark, but only a strangled sound came out. The pencil and clipboard dropped from his paws. Ignoring the chuckles of Top Dog, he looked around in desperation. Perhaps the Flock had already gone to the holding pen? He checked. It was empty. Maybe they had gone to gaze at the enormous squash? No.

Of course, he told himself. Shaun and the Flock would be getting some practice in before the trial started. Now that they had seen the competition, they would want to be in tip-top shape, ready to impress the judges. With hope in his heart and a paw shading his eyes, Bitzer looked across the sheepdog course . . .

The Flock wasn't there. And they weren't lining up for a cup of tea, or checking out **BARRY STILES'S** new range of **SOFT 'N' BOUNCY** sheep dips.

The sheep had completely disappeared. There was only one explanation: they must have been kidnapped by aliens! Bitzer glanced up at the sky. It was empty except for one or two fluffy clouds and a few circling seagulls.

From behind him came another snigger, and a scornful woof from Top Dog. What was Bitzer doing at a trial that had *real* sheepdogs? He couldn't even keep his flock in the right field.

Bitzer clenched his paws. Then a flash of familiar white fleece caught his eye.

Shaun was waving from the other side of the meadow. Nuts dived through a gap in the hedge next to Shaun. With a shake of his tail, Nuts was gone.

For a second, Bitzer could only stare, horrified, as Hazel, too, disappeared through the gap, then Timmy, followed by his mum.

The Twins were now wriggling through the hedge. Bitzer flapped his arms, barking as he ran across the field. Stop! STOP!

The Flock ignored him. After the Twins had squirmed through, Shirley shouldered her way into the hedge but soon got stuck. Putting his hooves on her bottom, Shaun shoved her through, then turned back to blow a raspberry at Bitzer. The sheep weren't interested in yet another boring sheepdog

00000.52

trial—they were off to have some fun at the seaside!

Shaun gave Bitzer a mischievous grin, but it quickly became a frown when he saw Top Dog howling with laughter and using his eHerder to take photos of the Flock running away.

The frown on Shaun's face became a scowl. No one laughed at Bitzer except him.

And the rest of the Flock.

And the Farmer.

And the chickens.

And the ducks, pigs, and Mower Mouth the goat.

And occasionally the pizza delivery boy.

But definitely *not* flashy-looking sheepdogs who thought they were as cool as a fridge full of cucumbers just because they had a fancy hat and a few silly contraptions.

Shaun glanced at the gap in the hedge,
then back at Bitzer, who crossed his arms and
tipped a paw. The message was clear: *What
did Shaun think he was up to?*

A new thought crossed Shaun's mind: if Bitzer lost the Flock at an actual *sheepdog trial*, it would make the Farmer a laughingstock too. He'd go red-faced and start shouting, like when he caught Mower Mouth eating his underwear last week. But this would be worse.

In his mind, Shaun saw the Farmer snatching away Bitzer's clipboard and whistle and ordering him into a van—a van that would take him away.

The picture faded. It was replaced by an image of the Farmer welcoming a new sheepdog. A sheepdog with sunglasses and an eHerder.

Shaun sighed. He wasn't going to enjoy the seaside after all. There would be no beach chair or drink in a coconut shell with umbrellas for him. If he didn't help Bitzer get the Flock back, soon they'd all be wearing electric earrings and trotting around the farm by remote control.

Feeling guilty, Shaun gave Bitzer a sheepish shrug—*sorry*—and tipped his head toward the seaside with a bleat. They needed to follow the rest of the Flock, and quickly.

Bitzer barked in irritation. How could Shaun invite him to the beach at a time like this? He was about to become known as the worst sheepdog since Two-Legged Licky, who herded his flock around and around in a circle at every sheepdog trial.

Rolling his eyes, Shaun shook his head. He pointed toward the Farmer, who had a teacup in one hand and a drooping egg sandwich in the other. The Farmer was surrounded by other farmers, all of them happily shouting "Blahblahblah" at one another. It would be a while before he realized that anything was wrong.

Shaun put his hooves to his lips and whistled a sheepdog command. If he and Bitzer worked together, they would have time to round up the Flock.

Bitzer blinked. Really? He jogged across the field to join Shaun.

Shaun nodded and tapped his wrist. They didn't have much time. If they were going to get back before the trial started, they had to

hurry. His jaw set with new resolve, Bitzer
dived through the hedge.

The chase was on!

CHAPTER THREE

I DO LIKE TO BLEAT BESIDE THE SEASIDE

Shaun emerged from the other side of the hedge to find Bitzer standing in a meadow on tiptoe and shading his eyes, panting eagerly. In the distance, the sea glittered, and—in the middle of the meadow—a young couple sat frozen with shock beside a picnic blanket.

Bitzer woofed at Shaun: *Which way?*

Shaun dropped to all four hooves and trotted toward the young couple. As he had suspected, the blanket was covered in hoof-prints as well as the trampled remains of a picnic. The young woman was still staring, wide-eyed, across the field. Her fingers were raised halfway to her mouth as if she had just been about to take a bite of something—delicious cake, perhaps?—that had been snatched away just before it reached her mouth.

Shaun nodded to himself: Shirley had definitely been here.

A few yards away was a swinging gate, and on the other side of the gate was a path that led down toward the seaside town and the beach beyond. Shaun bleated over his shoulder to Bitzer. *They went this way.*

Bitzer marched across the meadow, striding over the picnic blanket between the surprised couple. Shaun followed, stopping only long enough to help himself to a cheese, lettuce, and coleslaw sandwich from their picnic basket.

Tasty

He caught up with Bitzer at an old wooden signpost that read **PIDDLINGTON-ON-SEA.** Shaun checked a bush nearby. Sure enough, a few wisps of white wool were caught in its thorns; the Flock had headed straight toward the town. Dragging Bitzer by the elbow, he set off at a fast trot down the footpath.

A few minutes later, Shaun shook a fist at a passing cow and wiped cow pie from his hoof. Bitzer pointed out a rickety gate that had been flattened — another sure sign that Shirley had come this way.

They scrambled over the broken wood and skidded to a halt at the top of a hill.

Bitzer made a noise that sounded like "eeek." Shaun nodded in agreement, his heart sinking.

Below them was a bustling town. A crowded pier stretched out into the sea. There were a fair and a circus, fishing nets and

beach shops, and stalls selling hot dogs, rock candy, and fish and chips. Finding a handful of sheep here would be like trying to find . . . Shaun thought about it. . . . Well, it would be like trying to find an **actual** chocolate raisin in Nuts's bag of chocolate raisins.

Bitzer gave a low growl: *Come on.* Time was ticking on, and they had to try, or the Farmer would be laughed out of the farm show. With a gulp, Shaun trotted down the hill.

A few minutes later, the two peered out of a back alley onto Piddlington-on-Sea's main street. There was no sign of the Flock among the crowds, but a brightly colored ice-cream truck caught Shaun's eye. Whistling quietly, he began edging away from Bitzer toward it.

A woof brought him to a stop. Bitzer gave him a stern look. There was no time for ice cream.

Shaun edged back to Bitzer's side, trying to look innocent.

Bitzer rubbed his chin and stared into the crowd. Where should they start looking? Where would the sheep head first? Each sheep would want to do something different. If Bitzer could just figure out what it was, he'd know where to look.

Bitzer squeezed his eyes closed, thinking hard. He'd start with Shirley. What would Shirley most like to do? Perhaps she'd enjoy a game of beach volleyball? Or a brisk swim? Bitzer shook his head. No, that wasn't it. What did Shirley *love* doing . . . ?

Shaun tugged at his arm.

Bitzer flapped a paw at him. He was busy.

Did Shirley love . . . hang gliding? No . . . scuba diving? No . . .

Shaun tugged again.

Bitzer's eyes snapped open. Annoyed, he woofed at Shaun. If he wasn't allowed to think, they would never find—

Bleating, Shaun pointed. At the end of the busy street was a low wall that separated the pavement from the beach. Just visible over the top was a fluffy white fleece.

One of the Flock was sunbathing on the other side of that wall.

Bitzer sighed with relief—thinking was *really* difficult—and patted Shaun on the back: *Good work.* All they had to do now was make sure that the sheep didn't get away.

Shaun bleated. *He needed a disguise.* He didn't want any humans trying to take him back to the field before he had rounded up the Flock.

Moments later, Shaun and Bitzer strolled from the alley. Shaun was wearing a **KISS ME QUICK** hat Bitzer had found in a trash can and a pair of neon sunglasses someone had dropped.

They made their way toward the wall.

The fleece on the other side hadn't moved.

Bitzer gave Shaun a questioning look: *Ready?*

Shaun nodded.

Bitzer motioned three, two, one . . .

Together they leapt over the wall, spread-eagled, to grab the sheep.

Shaun landed with an oof, holding tight to the thick fleece. He frowned. The wool felt odd. It was softer and fluffier than normal. Perhaps, he thought, this sheep had been using the **BARRY STILES'S SOFT 'N' BOUNCY.**

If so, it was very good. And it smelled amazing. He'd have to remember to give it a try.

Bitzer landed next to him in the fleece. He grinned at Shaun. *One sheep down. Soon they would be on their way back to the*

A scream split the air. Shaun and Bitzer clung on tightly as the sheep started running in circles on the sand, still squealing loudly. A man wearing swimming trunks leapt to his feet. "Oiwharraflippinheck," he snarled.

Shaun and Bitzer leaned over the side of the fleece and looked down.

A screaming woman with white curls blinked up at them. They hadn't captured a stray member of the Flock; they had captured an old lady's fluffy white hairdo!

They jumped off and grinned apologetically, backing away from the old lady and her husband.

GRRRRR!

..Nudge...Nudge..

Shaun nudged Bitzer and pointed back over the wall. A white fleece bobbed past. It *had* to be one of the Flock this time. Together they turned tail and leapt back over the wall.

Shaun gave Bitzer a satisfied smirk as he landed. This time they had definitely caught—

"EEEEEK, FLYING SHEEEP! MUUUUUUM!"

With a gulp, Shaun looked down.

He had caught a small boy's cotton candy.

CHAPTER FOUR

FIND THE FLOCK

Bleating a summery tune to herself, Timmy's Mum strolled along the beach with the sun warming her curlers. She paused to wave at Timmy, who sat happily on his surfboard as it skimmed down a massive wave. A second later, disaster struck . . . the board flipped into the air, sending Timmy high into the sky.

SPLOOSH

Timmy's Mum sighed with relief and strolled on. Timmy was safe with the Twins. It was a lovely day for a walk on the beach—and what was this?

A woman was snoring in a deckchair. She had a dandelion puff of pink hair and the most amazing green sunglasses Timmy's Mum had ever seen. They were shaped like wings and dotted with jewels. They were *beautiful*.

Timmy's Mum held her breath. The woman was asleep; surely she wouldn't notice if someone borrowed them, just for a little while?

At the sound of a low bleat, the woman with pink hair jolted awake. A sheep wearing curlers and very familiar sunglasses stared back at her.

The sheep grinned.

The woman opened her mouth to scream, but then changed her mind and chuckled to herself. What a strange dream, she thought. A sheep couldn't afford sunglasses like that. And anyway, they would look *ridiculous* with curlers.

A second later, the woman started snoring again.

Timmy's Mum strolled on, enjoying the admiring looks she received for her new sunglasses.

Out at sea, Timmy was standing on the Twins' shoulders as they zigzagged across the waves on their water skis. When their speedboat curved in toward the beach, they let go of the towline, shooting over the water and coming to a gentle stop on the sand.

Timmy squeaked, jumping up and down. *Again! Again!*

Meanwhile, in the middle of town, Bitzer and Shaun wandered past street musicians singing and a magician . . . but no sheep. Bitzer glanced up at the town hall clock. His tail drooped. The sheepdog trial would start in less than an hour.

They had searched the shops (stopping so that Shaun could send a postcard to the pigs back at Mossy Bottom Farm), the games arcade (pausing so that Shaun could play the Evil Ducks III video game), and the fair (waiting so Shaun could ride the Terrifying Discombobulator of Death). But they hadn't found a single sheep. On top of everything else, fish and chips and wisps of cotton candy were stuck to his coat.

Bitzer groaned. Maybe Top Dog was

right. Maybe he *was* a useless sheepdog. . . .

Picking cotton candy from his fleece, Shaun nibbled it thoughtfully and nudged Bitzer. He pointed toward a line of bored-looking donkeys, then clip-clopped his hooves together. He shaded his eyes and peered around. If they were riding a donkey, they could get around the town more quickly *and* see over the heads of the crowd.

Bitzer nodded eagerly — what a *brilliant* idea . . . But he woofed in disappointment a second later when he noticed a sign: **A RIDE COSTS FIVE DOLLARS.** Where would he and Shaun find the money?

Shaun snickered and held up a hoof. Bitzer could leave this to him. The street performers had given him an idea.

Shaun launched into a dance, hooves tip-tapping on the pavement.

"Oooooo," said a voice in the crowd. A woman had stopped to stare. Shaun tap-danced over to her, twirled her around, and dipped her backward.

After planting a sloppy kiss on her cheek, he danced away. Bitzer held out his woolly hat. With a chuckle, the woman fished around in her purse and then dropped a coin in.

By now, a crowd was forming. Puffing and panting, Shaun danced harder, hooves clattering over the pavement, before dropping to one knee with his arms spread. Now *that* was entertainment!

The audience broke into applause, yelling for more. Bitzer's hat jingled as it filled with coins. Shaun grinned. He bowed and tapped a hoof, ready for another number. Then he bleated in protest as Bitzer yanked him away.

After pouring a heap of loose change into the surprised donkey owner's hands, Bitzer pointed to the biggest donkey. She was wearing a bridle that said **SWEET GERTRUDE.**

Shaun blinked nervously. Sweet Gertrude didn't look very sweet at all. In fact, she was glaring at them with a nasty gleam in her eye. Shaun gulped and looked around. Maybe **ADORABLE MAVIS** would be a better choice?

Bitzer shook his head. Sweet Gertrude looked like she was built for speed. He jumped into the saddle and pulled Shaun up behind him. Then Bitzer dug his heels into her flanks with a loud woof. Go! Fly like the wind, Sweet Gertrude.

Sweet Gertrude gave her riders a chilly stare and set off toward the beach at a very slow walk.

Shaun sighed and pinched the donkey's bottom. "EEEEEEE-AWWWW," Sweet Gertrude cried, rearing up and bolting. Clinging to the saddle, Shaun waved his **KISS ME QUICK** hat at the crowd. *This* was more like it.

Darting away from Gertrude's galloping hooves, shrieking sunbathers were covered by clouds of sand. Bitzer held on for dear life as she shot across the sand like a comet.

Shaun bleated urgently. Bitzer followed Shaun's pointing hoof. Strolling along the shore was a figure wearing outrageous sunglasses. She had curlers in her hair.

Timmy's Mum!

And there were Timmy and the Twins. They had made a scale model of the Eiffel Tower out of sand.

Bitzer barked loudly. Timmy's Mum looked up. Blinking, she pulled the sunglasses down on her nose and peered over the top of them. No, she thought to herself. It couldn't be . . .

Could it?

Timmy's Mum's eyes widened as she watched a donkey carrying Bitzer and Shaun on its back thundering toward her. She grabbed Timmy in panic. With the Twins at her heels, she began running up the beach.

Ears streaming out behind him and woofing in terror, Bitzer clung to Sweet Gertrude's mane as she smashed through the Twins' Eiffel Tower.

This was *not* the best way to herd sheep!

CHAPTER FIVE
ROUND THEM UP

Shirley's head poked through a cutout poster of a sheep wearing a bikini. Fluttering her eyelashes, she puckered her lips.

Click.

She gave a bleat of approval. This was exactly the sort of photo she had seen in the fashion pages of *Celebrity Sheep* magazine.

As she wandered away down the pier, Shirley beamed around at the staring crowds. She was having a wonderful time.

She stopped suddenly, her mouth watering. A little farther up the pier was a stall selling ice cream. With her tongue poking out of the corner of her mouth in concentration, she dug around in her fleece. There was some money in there somewhere, she was sure.

There. She pulled out a rubber chicken, frowned at it, and threw it over her shoulder before reaching in again. A broken kettle bounced across the pier. Finally, she found a purse.

Now she had to decide whether she wanted the Super-Whippy Double-Fudge Cone, or the Ten-Scoop Tower of Yum, or the Sprinkle-Covered Choco Gigantium with three extra scoops and a twizzle stick. But there was also the Tutti-Frutti Mega-Cone. . . .

It was too difficult to decide. She tutted to

herself. She would just have to take them all.

Bleating to get the ice-cream man's attention, she pressed her nose up against first one picture and then another while pushing the purse across the counter.

The ice-cream man wiped a hand across his forehead. It was a hot day, he told himself. He must have gotten too much sun. A very large sheep with a purse seemed to be trying to tell him that it wanted to buy *all* the ice-cream cones.

Wishing he had worn a sun hat—he clearly had sunstroke—he closed his eyes. If he counted to ten, the sheep would go away.

He'd made it to five—and Shirley had started banging the purse on the counter—when he opened his eyes again. In the distance, someone had started screaming. A second later, *everyone* was screaming.

Squealing people ran down the pier. Behind them galloped a dog and a sheep on  a plunging, rearing donkey. They seemed to be herding four other sheep.

Counting to ten wasn't going to do any good, the ice-cream man decided. What he needed was to lie down in a dark room, with an ice pack on his head.

Waving his hands—which Shirley thought was a sign for her to help herself—he ran, yelling, to the edge of the pier and jumped over the edge. He hit the water with a splash and began swimming for shore.

Shirley didn't need telling twice. Ignoring the screams behind her, she eagerly started stuffing her fleece with ice-cream cones. What a nice man, she thought to herself.

Then Shirley looked up to see a large, rearing donkey, and her mouth flopped open. Bitzer and Shaun were on the donkey's back, silhouetted against the sun.

Shaun bleated and dropped a rope around Shirley's neck. *Gotcha! One more sheep found.*

Shirley continued stuffing ice creams into her fleece as Sweet Gertrude gave a loud "HEEEE-HOOOORR." Hooves clattering on the pier, the donkey set off at a gallop. Shirley held on tight to the ice-cream stall, but it was no good—she was dragged along the pier.

Over the noise of screams and galloping hooves and an ice-cream stall collapsing, Shaun bleated urgently. Bitzer had seen it too; he pulled Sweet Gertrude's left ear.

Up ahead, a fluffy white tail disappeared into a tent. Outside was a sign . . .

Inside, Hazel held out a hoof. A frown crossed the wrinkled face of Madame Mist, Mystic Mistress. She had seen a lot of palms in her time, but never one like this. Not that it mattered, she told herself. She couldn't really read palms, or crystal balls, or tea leaves.

She just made it up as she went along. As long as she told her customers that a dashing stranger on a horse was coming to sweep them off their feet, they all went away happy.

Muttering under her breath, Madame Mist leaned in to scrape sand and mud off Hazel's hoof.

"Oooodashinstranger," she mumbled.

Hazel's ears pricked up. She couldn't understand what Madame Mist was saying, but she hoped it was something about being swept off her feet by a dashing stranger.

"Onnaorse," Madame Mist muttered.

At that moment, a group of bleating sheep, with Timmy's Mum in the lead, crashed through the flap of the tent. They were followed by an insane donkey.

Shaun just had time to tip his hat to Madame Mist before Gertrude galloped away,

chasing the Flock—and Hazel—through the canvas wall.

As the tent collapsed on top of her, Madame Mist smiled to herself. Her customer had been swept away by a dashing stranger. And a donkey was *nearly* a horse.

Maybe, she thought to herself. Maybe she did have the power to see the future after all.

Chapter Six

BIG TOP FLOCK

Nuts wriggled his bottom into a ringside seat between two ladies under the circus big top. With a rustle of his paper bag, he offered around some of the chocolate-covered raisins he'd found in the rabbit hutch.

"Mmmmlicious," one of the ladies said, fluttering her eyelashes and smiling at the funny-looking man in his thick woolly hat and sweater as she took a handful.

A second later, she spat chocolate-covered raisins into the circus ring. Choking, she turned to Nuts and gave him a cold glare.

Nuts smiled and shook the bag. *Would she like some more?*

The lady scowled, shifting away from him on the bench.

With a shrug, Nuts helped himself to the contents of the bag. People were strange, he thought, scooping chocolate-covered raisins into his mouth.

He munched for a few seconds, then frowned. Something wasn't right.

The chocolate-covered raisins were nice and chewy, but the flavor wasn't quite what he had been expecting. In a strange way, they tasted a little bit . . . he thought about it . . . well, *rabbity.*

Shrugging again, he shoved another hoof-ful into his mouth as the lights went down. He was going to see a show, after all,

and *what* a show! The pictures on the poster outside promised acrobats, jugglers, clowns, and a tabby cat leaping through a ring of fire.

Nuts bleated with excitement; he could hardly wait.

Nuts sat up in his seat, chocolate-covered raisins dropping from his open mouth. Bitzer and the Flock had joined the circus! And no one had asked him!

It was chaos in the ring. The ringmaster cracked his whip again and again, but no one took any notice.

Timmy's Mum was now wobbling around the ring on a ball with Timmy on her shoulders. The Twins were doing star

jumps and somersaults on the trampoline.

Hazel peered curiously into the mouth of a large cannon. Timmy's Mum rolled past, bleating loudly and accidentally knocking Hazel inside. A second later, with a huge bang,

Hazel shot out, legs scrabbling at the air as she sailed across the big top.

Meanwhile, Shaun was swinging backward and forward, clinging to the pant leg of one of the trapeze artists. There was a ripping sound.

The audience drew a deep breath— *oooh!*—as Shaun and Bitzer fell into a net below, somersaulted, and landed in a heap in front of the ringmaster.

He stared at them, red-faced with fury, and cracked his whip menacingly. The show was ruined.

An unexpected sound echoed around the big top. It came from the crowd. The ringmaster looked up in surprise. Everyone was standing up, stamping, cheering, laughing, and shouting for more. With a confused smile breaking out on his face, the ringmaster bowed.

Another cheer rocked the big top. Shaun looked up, openmouthed, as Nuts jumped

through a ring of fire and spread his arms: *Ta-dah!* If the Flock was going to join the circus, he wasn't going to be left out!

Dazed, Shaun shook his head. The sheepdog trial would be starting any minute. Plus, the circus performers were glaring at the Flock. Obviously, they didn't like being upstaged by a bunch of sheep. The Flock had to leave . . . *NOW!*

Shaun pulled Bitzer to his feet and pointed at the clowns' car. They'd get back to the **GREAT PIDDLINGTON-ON-SEA ANNUAL FARM EXTRAVAGANZA** in no time if they borrowed that.

The Flock was busy waving and dropping curtsies to the cheering crowd when a tiny car honked to a halt in front of them. Bitzer was hunched over the steering wheel. He glared up at them and jerked a thumb over his shoulder: *Get in!*

Timmy's Mum shook her head. They were stars! They owed it to the audience to do one more trick.

She bleated as Shaun jumped out and began shoving her and the rest of the grumbling Flock into the backseat as fast as he could. Sheep legs and heads stuck out of every window. With a heave, Shaun managed to squeeze Shirley in and then jumped into the passenger seat, giving Bitzer a thumbs-up.

The little car revved loudly. Shaun hung

out the window, waving to the crowd, as Bitzer hit the accelerator. Wheels spun. The car leapt forward and made it almost halfway across the circus ring before the doors fell off. Then the wheels. Finally, the hood flipped off in a puff of smoke and spun across the tent.

The crowd roared.

With the ringmaster leading them, the circus performers were closing in. The clowns looked especially unhappy. The car was their best joke, and the sheep had ruined it!

Shaun looked at Bitzer. Bitzer looked at Shaun.

There was only one thing left to do: *RUN!*

CHAPTER SEVEN
THE FINAL SHOWDOWN

After wiping sweat from his forehead, Bitzer closed the gate of the holding pen on a flock of panting sheep. Pheww! They'd made it, and just in time. A familiar figure strode across the meadow.

"Gerronwithitthen," barked the Farmer. Why was Bitzer leaning on the gate and generally lazing about? It was nearly his turn to herd sheep in the competition. Why wasn't he ready?

After snapping off a smart salute, Bitzer swung the gate open again as the Farmer stamped away. One by one, he checked off the sheep on his clipboard — Shaun in a **KISS ME QUICK** hat: *Check*. Shirley, looking grumpy: *Check*. The Twins, both glaring at him: *Check*. Timmy's Mum, giving him an icy look over the top of her rather fabulous sunglasses . . .

Bitzer's pencil stopped mid-check as he removed Timmy's Mum's sunglasses.

He looked around at a sea of angry sheep. Apart from Shaun, none of them looked like they were raring to go out and win the **GREAT PIDDLINGTON-ON-SEA ANNUAL FARM EXTRAVAGANZA GOLD CUP FOR BEST SHEEPDOG.**

Bitzer scratched his head and gave Shaun a questioning look. Where was the Flock's team spirit? He barked, pointing to the gleaming gold cup. Where was their eagerness to win a

glorious victory and return to Mossy Bottom
Farm in triumph? He punched the air. This
was a day that would go down in *history* —

Timmy blew a raspberry at him.

"Wh-wh-whuff?" Bitzer looked from face
to face. What was wrong?

Hazel bleated and pointed back toward
the seaside, then turned her back and folded
her arms. The message was clear: the Flock
had been having a nice day at the seaside until
Shaun and Bitzer had ruined everything.
Bitzer could find some other sheep to herd.
The Flock was on strike!

Timmy's Mum nodded in agreement. Timmy hadn't eaten any ice cream or gone on any of the fair rides, *and* he'd wanted to go shark fishing. And now Bitzer had taken her sunglasses too.

One by one the sheep turned away.

The pencil dropped from Bitzer's paw. He gulped, looking from the Farmer, to the sheepdog trial course — where Top Dog was

tapping his eHerder and perfect lines of sheep were trotting into a pen—to Shaun. Help!

Bleating quietly, Shaun tried to persuade the Flock. If Bitzer couldn't herd the sheep out of the starting pen, it would be worse than if he'd lost them! Everyone would laugh. The Farmer would be madder than Sweet Gertrude.

As one, the Flock shrugged. They weren't listening.

In the field, Top Dog held up the eHerder. *Tap, tap, tap.* His buzzing sheep trotted through gates, around hurdles, and into pens. With a last twiddle of the machine, he guided his flock into the final pen. Ears drooping sadly, the last sheep carefully locked the gate behind herself.

A round of applause spread across the meadow. The judges' scores were good: 9.9, 9.9, 10. Shaun's stomach lurched as he saw the Farmer pull an eHerder brochure from his pocket and start flicking through the pages.

Looking even more smug than usual, Top Dog waggled his eyebrows at Bitzer. *Beat that with your whistle and clipboard.*

Shaun had to do something. He turned to the Flock. How could he change their minds? Then he saw a scrap of fabric from the trapeze artist's pants caught in his hoof. Of course! The Flock had loved the circus, and the audience had loved the Flock's tricks. He took a deep breath, then bleated loudly.

It was time to show the **GREAT PIDDLINGTON-ON-SEA ANNUAL FARM EXTRAVAGANZA** what the Mossy Bottom Flock could do!

The sheep looked at one another, bleating quietly. They *had* enjoyed being in the circus . . .

Timmy's Mum shook her head.

Shaun gave her a winning smile. If the Flock won, there would be ice cream for Timmy, and for everyone else too.

Timmy bounced up and down in excitement. Ice cream? *Really?*

Shaun nodded.

Hazel peered at Shaun suspiciously. *How was he going to get ice cream?*

Shaun tapped the side of his nose. It was a secret. But if the Flock wanted ice cream, it would have to beat Top Dog, and *that* would be difficult.

A judge opened the gate. Bitzer's turn had come.

"Oooombye," the Farmer mumbled, and went back to reading his brochure.

Bitzer turned to the Flock. He barked pleadingly and held up the clipboard: **HERDING PATTERN BITZER BRAVO.** Please, please, *please* . . .

In a wave of jumping, spinning, rolling sheep, Bitzer was swept around the course, whistle blasting and arms waving as he gave directions.

Teacups dropped from farmers' hands. The crowd spilled out of the tent that housed the enormous squash to gawk at how amazingly well trained the Farmer's animals were.

Finally, the Flock arrived at the pen in front of the panel of judges. Cartwheeling and backflipping, the Flock raced in.

As Bitzer's whistle gave a final peep, the sheep formed a pyramid, passing Bitzer up until he was standing on top. Then the sheep dropped down and trotted obediently into orderly lines.

The Farmer looked up from the brochure to see the judges leap to their feet. Cheering,

they held up their scores: 10, 10, and 10. He
stared at his eHerder brochure for a moment,
then tossed it into a trash can.

CHAPTER EIGHT

SHEEP BY THE SEA

As the car bounced across the meadow, Shaun looked back and grinned. In the distance he could see a red-faced farmer shouting at Top Dog. The farmer grabbed the eHerder from the sheepdog's paw and stomped on it. Behind them, Top Dog's flock bleated and cheered.

Shaun turned away, still smiling. Up ahead, the Farmer's head was bouncing against the roof and Bitzer had his head out the window, an enormous gold cup resting in his lap. Everything had turned out all right.

A chorus of bleats interrupted his thoughts. Turning, he found the Flock staring at him. Hazel held out a hoof and bleated again. Shaun had promised them ice cream! It was time to pay up.

Shaun grinned. Remembering how Shirley had hidden the ice cream in her fleece on the pier, he stuck a hoof into her fleece, rummaged around, and pulled out a Super-Whippy Double-Fudge Cone, then a Sprinkle-Covered Choco Gigantium with three extra scoops and a twizzle stick. There was enough ice cream in Shirley's fleece for everyone, and it was only slightly melted!

Soon, all the sheep were licking happily at their huge cones while the trailer jolted and clattered along the country lane.

Shirley reached into her fleece and helped herself to a Tutti-Frutti Mega-Cone. Luckily, she had brought enough for seconds, and thirds, and fourths.

Nuts shook a paper bag. Did anyone want to sprinkle chocolate-covered raisins on their ice cream? They were delicious, once you got used to the flavor.

A few minutes later, the Farmer jerked the wheel and jammed on the brakes, almost throwing the sheep out of the trailer.

Ahead was a small bay. Sparkling waves lapped against the shore. Swallowing the last of his ice cream, Shaun gave a wide smile.

The Farmer jumped down from the truck and slammed the door.

He'd rolled his pants up around his knees and had a knotted hankie on his head. Under his arm was a beach chair. Setting off toward the shore, he jerked his thumb at the trailer. Bitzer could herd the sheep down to the sea for a swim. The Farmer was going to have an afternoon snooze on the beach.

Sheep bleating happily around him, Shaun gave Bitzer a thumbs-up. He dipped into Shirley's fleece one last time, pulling out a coconut shell with a small umbrella in it.

ACTIVITIES

WORD SEARCH

Can you find all the words listed below?
Don't wreck your book! Photocopy
this page first.

B	E	H	A	M	R	E	R	A	F
B	E	A	C	T	F	Z	T	B	A
I	R	I	E	H	E	R	D	E	R
T	A	R	E	S	F	D	O	A	M
Z	I	A	S	H	A	U	N	C	E
E	S	E	T	E	I	N	K	H	R
B	I	T	Z	E	R	S	E	A	N
E	N	K	E	P	K	E	Y	D	O

Sheep   Sea
Shaun   Beach
Bitzer   Farmer
eHerder   Donkey
Fair   Raisin

HOW TO DRAW TIMMY

MATERIALS

Pencil

A large sheet of paper

STEP 1 Draw a circle.

STEP 2 Add legs.
These are made up
of six lines and three
circles.

STEP 3 Give Timmy a head
by drawing another circle.
This time the circle should
be larger at the bottom
than the top.

STEP 4 Make Timmy's tail
by adding an oval shape.

STEP 5 Draw two
banana shapes
for Timmy's ears.

STEP 6 Give Timmy some eyes.
Then add his fleece.

How to Juggle

Materials

Three balls

(Each one should ideally be brightly colored and
about the size and weight of a lemon.)

STEP 1 With hands level and elbows bent at
90 degrees, practice throwing one ball from
hand to hand until you can do so easily
without having to reach to make a catch.
The throw should come from the forearm
rather than the wrist, and the ball should
pop from the palm of the hand instead
of rolling off the fingers.

STEP 2 To introduce a second ball, start with
a ball in each hand. Then toss one ball up.
As that ball begins to come down, throw the
second one and get ready to catch the first

ball with the same hand. The second ball should pass underneath the first.

STEP 3 Practice, practice, practice! Repeat steps 1 and 2 for as long as it takes to feel confident.

STEP 4 To add the third ball, take one ball in one hand and two balls in the other. Begin by throwing with the hand holding the single ball. Then, as before, throw the second ball as the first one is coming down. Then toss the third one as the second one is dropping, and so on.

STEP 5 Practice!